CUENTO DE LUZ

In memory of my *beloved* and *sadly missed* brother Miguel Ángel Calle,
a *sensitive soul* and great poet, who always supported me in my personal
and professional life. He was a generous person, always ready to help others.
He was my greatest friend, and I will always be in debt to him.

- Ramiro Calle -

To my dear friends, I dedicate this *beautiful song* of friendship. With love.

- Nívola Uyá -

Yoga in the Jungle

Text © Ramiro Calle
Illustrations © Nívola Uyá
This edition © 2014 Cuento de Luz SL
Calle Claveles 10 | Urb Monteclaro | Pozuelo de Alarcón | 28223 | Madrid | Spain
www.cuentodeluz.com
Title in Spanish: Yoga en la selva
English translation by Jon Brokenbrow

ISBN: 978-84-16078-16-5

Printed by Shanghai Chenxi Printing Co., Ltd. February 2014, print number 1410-4

FSC
www.fsc.org
MIX
Paper from
responsible sources
FSC® C007923

Yoga in the Jungle

Ramiro Calle • Nívola Uyá

*R*avi and Tony first met in the enormous hall of the United States Embassy in Delhi. They were both running and crashed into each other. They looked at each other with surprised, questioning expressions, each of them wondering what the other was doing there.

Ravi had very dark skin, hair as dark as jet stone, and glittering black eyes.

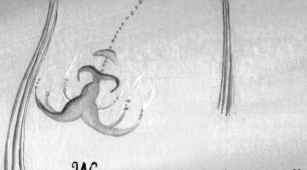

"Who are you?" asked Tony, still in a slightly dazed state.

"I'm Ravi," said the little Indian boy, his voice full of confidence. "That was quite a bump you gave me! What's your name?"

"I'm Tony, the ambassador's son. This is where I live."

"Well, I'm your gardener's grandson," replied Ravi, in a slightly mocking tone.

"You're the one who gave me a good bump," smiled Tony, who hardly ever had the chance to meet kids his age. "You're like a train!"

$\mathcal{R}$avi burst out laughing, as if he'd just heard the funniest thing in the world, while he waved his arms around and huffed and puffed like a steam train.

Suddenly, they stopped and looked at each other closely.

"Do you play baseball?" asked Tony.

"Here we play cricket," answered Ravi. "But you know what? I prefer the wisdom of the jungle!"

$\mathcal{T}$ony's eyes opened as wide as saucers. What was that about the wisdom of the jungle?

"Stop looking so surprised," said Ravi, chuckling to himself. "Haven't you ever heard about the secret of the jungle?"

"No, never. Can you tell me about it?"

"No, you can't talk about it."

"So?"

"So tomorrow, we're going to the jungle," said Ravi. "There are things you've got to experience that aren't for talking about."

*T*ony was thrilled about the chance to set off on an adventure, but a little worried too.

"We'll get in trouble," he said.

"So what?" Ravi asked boldly. "My grandfather always says that learning is just a part of us. Wherever we are, there is also learning."

Tony hesitated, but he was overwhelmed by his curiosity to discover the secret of the jungle.

"I'll leave a note for my grandfather, and you leave one for your parents, telling them you'll be back in two or three days and for them not to worry. I'll meet you tomorrow at dawn. Bring some money, but make sure they're rupees, not dollars. Don't let me down. The jungle's waiting for us!"

Just then, a huge, fluffy white cat with gleaming, yellow eyes bounced into the room and stared intently at the two little boys. "That's Emile, my cat," said Ravi proudly. "My grandfather says I must watch him all the time and I'll learn a lot from him. Cats are very mysterious and wise."

*T*hey met at dawn and quietly sneaked out of the embassy towards the railway station. Ravi haggled with a rickshaw driver who took them to the station, which was a solid mass of people. He bought their tickets for the cheapest passenger car, after skillfully cutting into the long, long queue. They climbed up into their car, but it was full to overflowing, and they only found a place in the corner to sit down. Tony looked at the women's bright, shining dresses.

Ravi saw him looking and said, "They're called saris. They're very, very long. And do you see that big guy in the corridor with a turban and a long beard? He's a Sikh. I'm a Hindu. There are lots of religions in India, but only one God."

After a few hours' journey, the train came to a halt at a station in the middle of a jungle. The boys jumped out and began to head into the trees.

"Don't be afraid," said Ravi, seeing the nervous expression on Tony's face. "My grandfather says that animals are the gentlest creatures there are. You have to keep your eyes and ears open. Look at this wonderful place!"

"Oh, there's a cobra!" he exclaimed.

Tony leapt backwards in fright.

"Don't be afraid!" laughed Ravi. "We are all one. That's yoga, our science of the spirit that goes back thousands of years. Come on, we're going to pretend to be the cobra!"

Ravi dropped to the ground and did

The cobra pose.

Tony followed him.

"Look, look!" he said, carefully looking around. "A locust! Let's pretend we're as tiny as he is!"

They both did *the locust pose*.

"This is fun!" said Tony, with a huge smile on his face.

"We are all one," said Ravi. "Feel your breath. The trees breathe, too. Look at that one. Isn't it beautiful? Come on, I'll show you

THE TREE POSE."

They did it together, although Tony found it quite difficult to keep his balance. They laughed. A cool, scented breeze wafted between the trees.

"Look, look!" exclaimed Ravi, who didn't miss a thing. "There's a huge crayfish. Look at his pincers! Come on, let's do

THE PINCER POSE."

Ravi showed Tony how to do it properly.

"If we do these poses, we don't just improve our bodies, but also our minds. Feel how you're stretching all of your muscles. Doesn't it feel great?"

"It really does!" said Tony, absolutely amazed. They kept walking until they reached an area of swampland.

"Oh! Look over there! There's a huge crocodile in the lagoon!" This time it was Tony who took the initiative. "Shall we imitate him?"

"Oh yes!" said Ravi. "Like my grandfather says, nature teaches us everything. All you need to do is watch it, be aware of it and experience it. But don't stop feeling how you breathe."

They did THE CROCODILE POSE and then kept walking.

The sun's rays shone through the dense tree cover. Suddenly they heard a loud trumpeting noise, and in the distance saw a wild elephant. They watched it, keeping perfectly still.

"Shall we copy him?" asked Tony, who was becoming more and more captivated by the wonders of nature.

"Yes, but hush, don't make any noise. Wait until he leaves."

The elephant plodded off quietly. Tony waved his arm in the air to say goodbye.

"Let's see if he comes back!" said Ravi, and then they did
the elephant pose.

Then they tried other different poses, which filled them with energy.

*T*he hours went by, and the sun gradually set. A huge, bright moon floated in the sky. Ravi finally showed his friend how to sit in

a meditation pose.

"Listen to the sound of the jungle. Feel the heartbeat of Mother Earth. Everything is sacred," whispered the little Hindu boy.

"The wisdom of the jungle is amazing," said Tony, absolutely thrilled.

"And the wisdom of the mountains, of the valleys, the rivers and the meadows!" laughed Ravi. "This is a wonderful planet, and we must respect it and take care of it."

They closed their eyes and felt as if they were one, at peace and full of happiness.

The adventure in the jungle, its wisdom and its secrets, brought them together as friends for the rest of their lives.